First published 1992 by Walker Books Ltd
87 Vauxhall Walk, London SE11 5HJ

This edition published 2009

2 4 6 8 10 9 7 5 3 1

© 1992 Helen Oxenbury

The right of Helen Oxenbury to be identified as author/illustrator
of this work has been asserted by her in accordance with the
Copyright, Designs and Patents Act 1988

This book has been typeset in Garamond Educational

Printed in China

British Library Cataloguing in Publication Data:
a catalogue record for this book is available from the British Library.

ISBN 978-0-7445-1262-5

www.walker.co.uk

Tom and Pippo on the beach

Helen Oxenbury

WALKER BOOKS

AND SUBSIDIARIES

LONDON · BOSTON · SYDNEY · AUCKLAND

One day Daddy and I
went to the beach in the car...

and of course Pippo
came as well.

Daddy said that the sun was really bright and I ought to wear my hat, because the sun might make me sick.

I said that it didn't seem
bright to me and I didn't
feel sick and anyway Pippo
needed to wear my hat.

Daddy said he would make a hat for Pippo so that I could wear my hat. He said he would make Pippo a hat out of newspaper

I said to Daddy,
"Look, Pippo doesn't
like the paper hat."

"I know! I'll wear it
and he can wear mine."

I'm glad Pippo's got the best hat, so he won't feel sick in the sun.